ORCHARD BOOKS

96 Leonard Street, London EC2A 4RH

Orchard Books Australia

14 Mars Road, Lane Cove, NSW 2066

ISBN 1 86039 159 1 (hardback)

ISBN 1 86039 992 4 (paperback)

First published in Great Britain 1997

First paperback publication 1998

Text © Geraldine McCaughrean 1997

Illustrations © Sophie Windham 1997

The right of Geraldine McCaughrean to be identified as the Author
and Sophie Windham as the Illustrator of this Work has been asserted by them
in accordance with the Copyright, Designs and Patents Act, 1988.

A CIP catalogue record for this book is available from the British Library.

Printed in Singapore

Unicorns! Unicorns!

Geraldine McCaughrean

Illustrated by Sophie Windham

 ORCHARD BOOKS

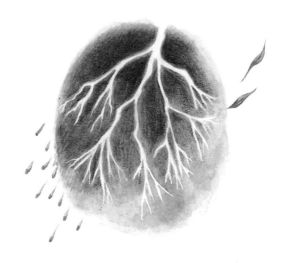

For Mo and John
G. McC.

For Nettie
S.W.

The day God decided to flood the world, the thunder clapped and the lightning cheered. The clouds drank up water off the wild wave-tops, then spilled it over the Earth. Noah felt the rain on his face and began to call: "Animals! Animals! Come aboard! The flood is coming!"

Some of the animals came at once. Some came quickly. Some had a long way to travel. Some, like the snails, moved slow as slow.

"Wait a little longer, dear," said Noah's wife. "The best beasts of all are not aboard yet: the Unicorns."

"And if we go without them," said his sons, "the world will lose its Unicorns for ever more."

But Noah had so little time. He looked at his lists:

Tarantulas

Terrapins

Tortoises

Turtles

Unicorns...

He went up to the prow of the Ark and blew his ramshorn trumpet.

He went down to the stern of the Ark and drummed his goatskin drum.

"Unicorns! Unicorns! Come aboard!" he called. "The fearful flood is coming!"

The Unicorns were far, far away, flicking the raindrops from the leaves of the jacaranda trees, making the air sparkle. Their manes ran down like milk, their tails like melting snow splashing over their silvery heels. They were playful, carefree creatures. But, as soon as they heard Noah call, they did set out for the Ark.

As they walked, they saw two Tortoises standing at the edge of a pool of water, too afraid to paddle across.

The Unicorns carried them over in their gentle white mouths.

"We must hurry and you must hurry," said the Tortoises, stumping on their way.

"You must hurry, yes," said one Unicorn, "but our legs are a little longer than yours."

"And though we should not boast," said the other, "God made us fast on our feet."

Mrs Noah and her sons stood along the rail of the Ark and shouted through the falling rain: "Unicorns! Unicorns! Come aboard!" The raindrops spattered the ground and made the soft soil run.

But the Unicorns were making their way towards the Ark. As they trotted along, they saw a little Deer mired in mud, struggling to free its spindly legs from the clinging, wet earth.

They knelt down and nudged it tenderly forwards, until it reached firmer ground.

"I must hurry, and you must hurry," said the Deer, still quivering with fright.

"You must hurry, yes," said one Unicorn, "but our legs are a little stronger than yours."

"And though we should not boast," said the other, "God made us fast on our feet."

On board the Ark, the animals were growing anxious.
The horses tossed their heads. The lions began to pace.
The tigers and ocelots let out a roar: "Unicorns! Unicorns!
Come aboard! The ground is covered in water, and the Flood
is nearly here!"

At that very moment, the Unicorns were dashing towards
the Ark. But as they galloped, a Butterfly, struck by an ice-cold
drop of rain, fell to the ground in front of them. Its wings were
soon waterlogged.

So one Unicorn picked it up on the tip of his tongue,
and the other breathed her warm breath on the papery wings
until they were dry.

"I must hurry, and you must hurry," said the Butterfly
fluttering into the air once more.

"You must hurry, yes," said one Unicorn, "before more
raindrops wet your wings. But our skins throw off the rain."

"And though we should not boast," said the other,
"God made us fast on our feet."

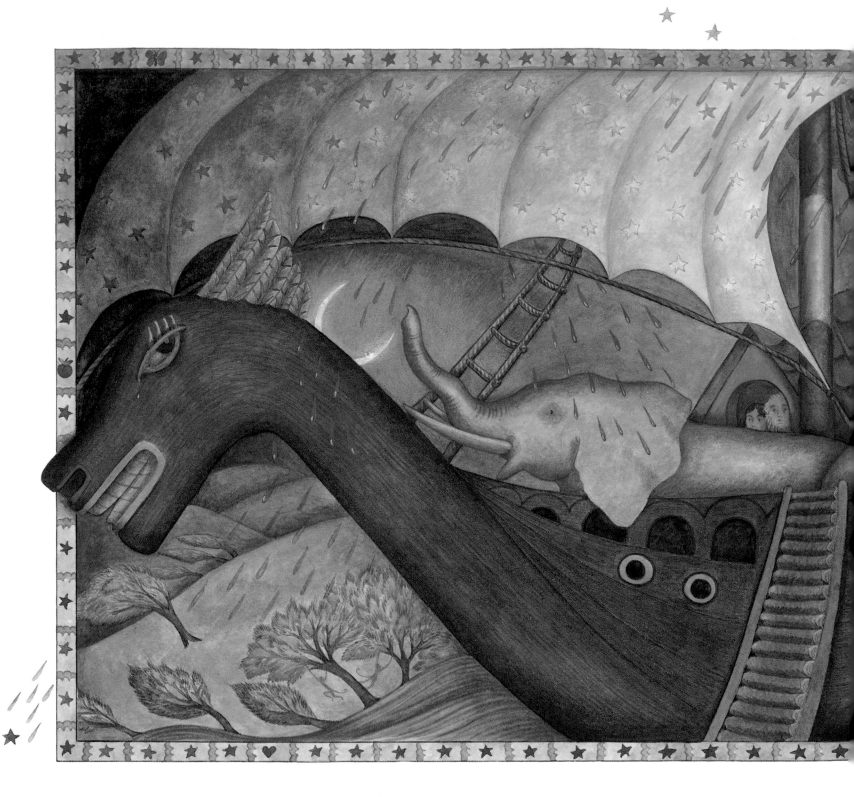

The water was rising fast. The Ark began to roll from side to side.
Noah said, "I can wait only till the clouds cover the sun."
The elephants trumpeted over the watery wastes: "Unicorns!
Unicorns! Come aboard!"

The Unicorns heard the elephants   who did not? – and lunged towards the Ark.

But as they reared and plunged through the numbing cold water, they saw two Monkeys still playing in the trees.

"Come down! Be quick, you foolish creatures!" called the Unicorns.
"Noah called you, and you should come when you are called!"

"Foh-fah!" said one. "Plenty of time! We're having fun!"

"Hee-hah!" said the other. "We can swing through the trees by our
tails and reach the Ark whenever we please. Plenty of time."

"But the trees are falling!" called the Unicorns. "The forests are
drowning. The water is rising and the sky is turning black!

Stop your playing, silly Monkeys, or Noah will go without you!"

"Go without us? Never!"

"Go without us? He wouldn't dare!"

But the Monkeys shivered in their treetop, and glanced towards the distant Ark. It was already afloat and drifting. "Wait for us! Wait for us!" screeched the Monkeys, and leapt through the treetops, hand over fist over tail.

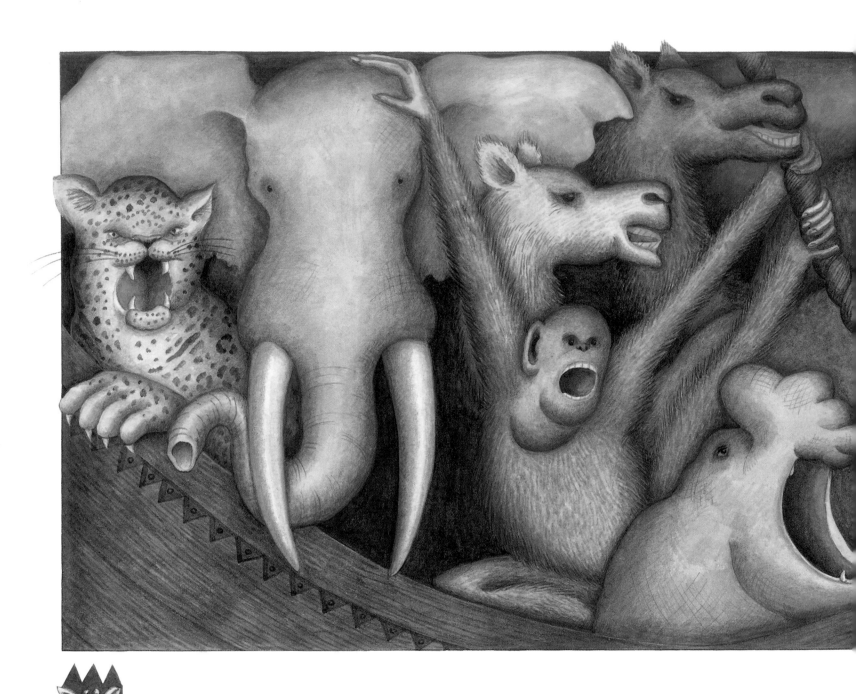

Then all the animals from stem to stern began to shout:
"Unicorns! Unicorns! Come aboard! Your legs are long,
but the Flood will be longer: forty days and forty nights."

They all called and bleated, squawked and roared, jibbered
and honked. They strained their necks over the wooden rails,
and shouted till the wet world echoed:
"UNICORNS! UNICORNS! COME ABOARD!"

As the two monkeys leapt aboard, Noah began to raise the gangplank.

"Wait, Father, wait!" cried his sons. Noah closed the windows against the driving rain.

"Wait, wait, Noah!" shouted the animals.

"I dare not. The Unicorns should have come when I called," said Noah, "but they were too silly."

"No, no! That was us!" shrieked the Monkeys, but Noah did not understand them.

"They travelled too slowly," said Noah.

"No, no!" cried the Tortoises, "that was us!" but Noah did not understand them.

"Since they are so beautiful, perhaps they stayed to admire themselves in the water," said Noah.

A Butterfly fluttered in his face —"No, no, that was me!"— but he brushed it away with one hand and shot the bolt on the door.

The floodwaters turned the great boat about and about, and the winds blew it on its way.

The Unicorns, swimming now, and out of their depth, beat on the planks with their snow-white hooves. But nobody heard them above the thunder.

Darkness fell, and rain clouds blotted out the moon.

But all night Noah and the animals wept salt tears, and all the birds were silent, because the Unicorns were lost to the world for ever.

For forty days and forty nights the clouds rained and the animals wept.

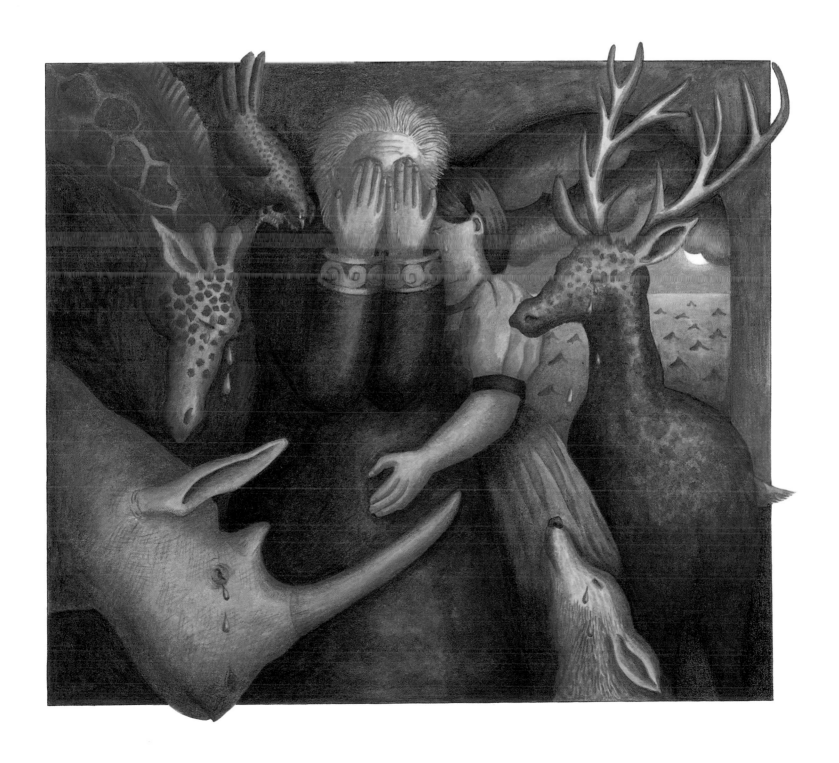

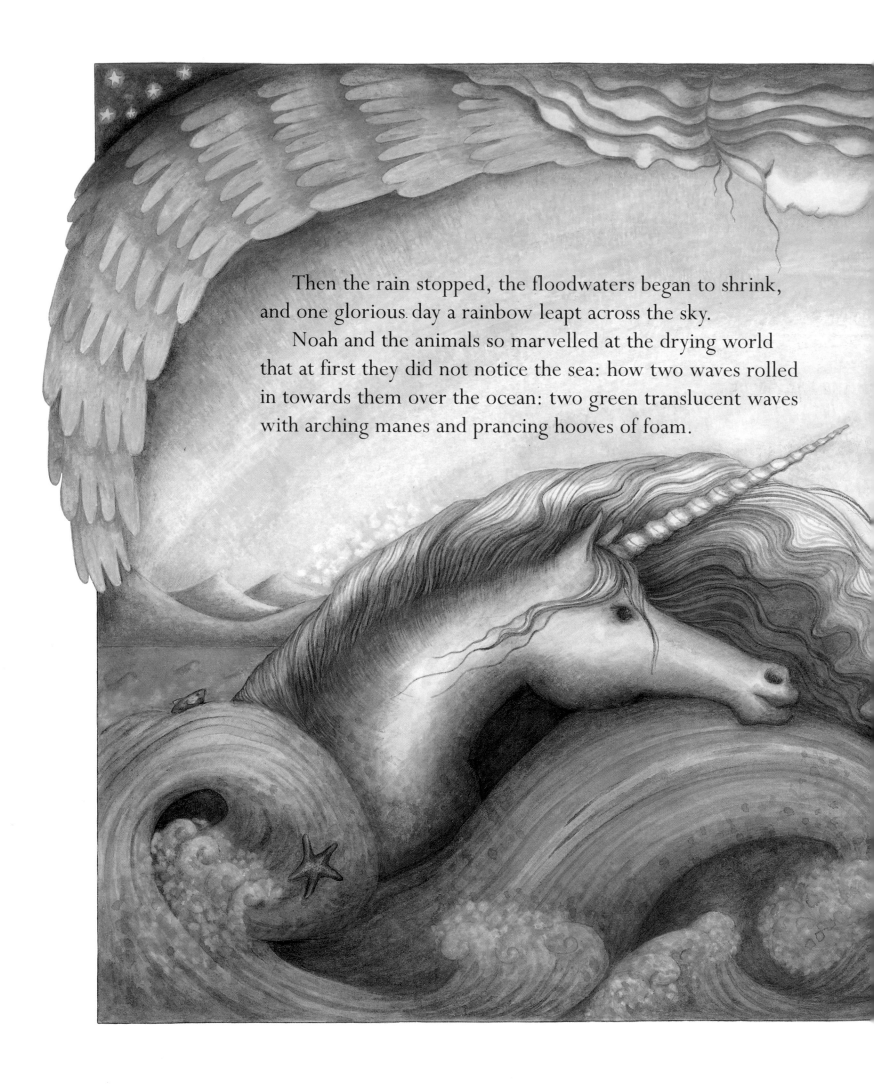

Then the rain stopped, the floodwaters began to shrink,
and one glorious day a rainbow leapt across the sky.
    Noah and the animals so marvelled at the drying world
that at first they did not notice the sea: how two waves rolled
in towards them over the ocean: two green translucent waves
with arching manes and prancing hooves of foam.

But when they did see they stretched their necks and cheered till the world echoed: "The Unicorns! The Unicorns are alive!"

Even through the driving rain, the angels must have seen who stopped to help the Deer and Tortoises. Even above the rolling thunder, the angels must have heard who called to the Monkeys, who breathed on the Butterfly.

Even now, between the breaking of waves,
you may sometimes hear the warm breathing of
the Unicorns close by.

Out at sea, on a stormy day, their countless
children prance on the wavetops, buck, and rear and
dance and leap – a fleet of white horses, fast of foot.

Though they race for dry land, they somehow
never reach it. Only their candy-twist horns and
sugar-stranded tails melt on the wet sand amid
the seaweed and shining shells.